For Nicola, Eliza,
Jack and Tom
A.M.

For Miles, with love
J.M.

Published in 1995 by Magi Publications
55 Crowland Avenue, Hayes, Middlesex UB3 4JP

Text © 1995 by Anne Mangan
Illustrations © 1995 by Joanne Moss

Printed and bound in Hong Kong

ISBN 1 85430 277 9 (Hardback)
ISBN 1 85430 125 X (Paperback)

Little Teddy Left Behind

by Anne Mangan

illustrated by Joanne Moss

MAGI PUBLICATIONS

London

Little Teddy woke up and sneezed loudly. Nobody heard him because there was no one there. Nicola and Jack had moved to a new house.

"I'm all alone," said Teddy. "They've left me behind. They never were very good at packing. I'm all dusty too," he said, and he sneezed and he sneezed.

It grew dark, and at last Teddy went to sleep again . . .

. . . until the next morning when the cleaning lady's dog spotted him and picked him up.

"What have you there?" asked the lady, and when she saw how grubby Teddy was, she grabbed him with her big hands . . .

. . . and popped him into the washing machine!

"Oh help!" cried Teddy, but nobody heard his tiny
little squeak.

It was dreadful in the washing machine. Teddy was
whirled round and round and washed and spun-dried.
He growled his very loudest growl, but nobody came to
rescue him. He spun round even faster until he was
quite dizzy. At last the machine stopped and Teddy lay there
among all the damp clothes.

The cleaning lady opened the machine door and took out Teddy. "You're not quite dry yet," she said.

"I'll do," growled Teddy, but she took no notice and pinned him upside-down on a clothesline.

"I'd rather be dirty and the right way up," he cried, but of course nobody heard his tiny squeak.

It was windy and Teddy swung about on the clothesline. It was exciting in a way, like flying in Space.

All at once the line broke, and Teddy fell off into the grass. Butterflies flew around him and bees buzzed over his head. Teddy liked the bright cheerful butterflies, but he was a bit afraid of the bees.

"You scare me," he squeaked, but the bees were too busy to hear him.

Suddenly Teddy felt hot breath in his ear.

"Oh no!" he cried. "It's that dog again!"

The dog seized the little bear in his big teeth and pushed through a very prickly hedge into the next garden.

"Oh my poor fur!" gasped Teddy.

A lady looked up as the dog rushed onto the lawn.

"Ugh, he's got a rat in his mouth!" she screamed and threw a gardening glove at them.

"I'm not a rat!" growled Teddy.

The dog ran out through the garden gate into a wood.

"Oh, I do wish he'd drop me," thought poor Teddy and luckily, at last, he did. The dog had spotted a rabbit and was off into the undergrowth, leaving Teddy behind.

Teddy lay very still, hoping the dog wouldn't come back. It was quiet in the wood – but not for long. Two children came rushing towards him.

"Hey, a little teddy!" cried one of the children.

"That's me," thought Teddy. "Now what?"

He soon found out.

"Catch!" the boy yelled and poor Teddy was tossed from one to the other until he felt quite sick.

"Can't they see I'm not a ball, stupid things!" he thought.

The children soon grew tired of their game and the girl flung Teddy away, high into the air.

Up, up, up he sailed, right into the branches of a tall tree. No sooner had he landed than he heard an angry chittering noise.

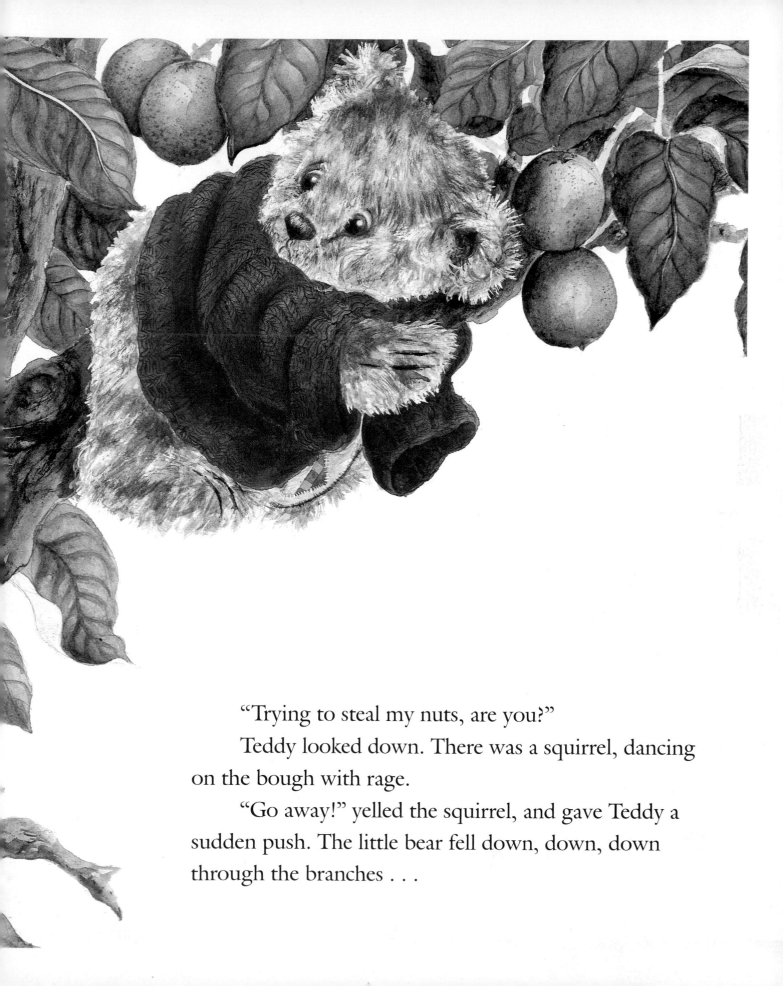

"Trying to steal my nuts, are you?"

Teddy looked down. There was a squirrel, dancing on the bough with rage.

"Go away!" yelled the squirrel, and gave Teddy a sudden push. The little bear fell down, down, down through the branches . . .

. . . and landed on a wooden floor.

He was lying there, getting his breath back and
worrying whether Jack and Nicola would ever find him
again, when he heard children's voices. He tried his growl
and he tried his squeak, but they were too small for
the children to hear him.

The floor was as dusty as the empty room he had
left behind. Once again Teddy began to sneeze and sneeze.
The sneeze was louder than the growl and the squeak, and at
last the voices came nearer . . .

"Look, there's a ladder!"

"It's a tree house!"

Two faces were peering at him – two faces he knew very well!

"It's Little Teddy!" cried Jack. "How did he get into our new garden? I thought he was all packed up."

"I don't know, but it doesn't matter," said Nicola, giving Teddy a hug. "We've found Teddy *and* a tree house."

"It's Teddy's tree house," said Jack. "He found it."

His very own house! Teddy liked the idea.

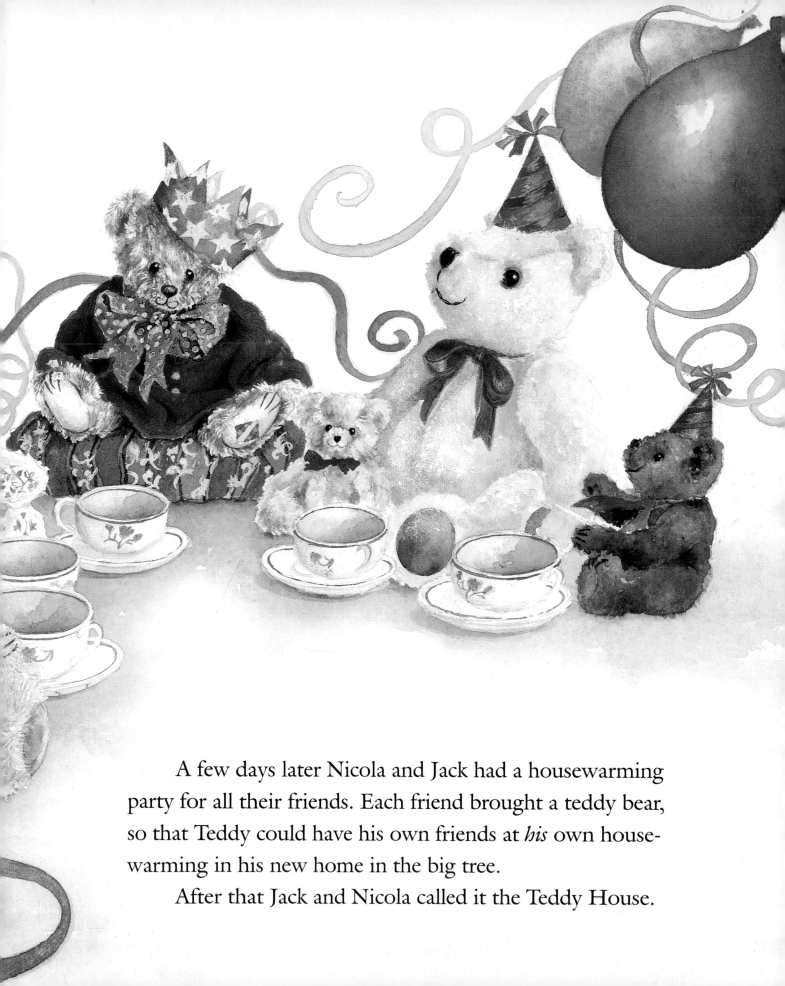

A few days later Nicola and Jack had a housewarming
party for all their friends. Each friend brought a teddy bear,
so that Teddy could have his own friends at *his* own housewarming in his new home in the big tree.

After that Jack and Nicola called it the Teddy House.